Dorothy M. Chapman
June 14, 1971
from
Oly, me and Don

Bright Horizons

ALSO BY HELEN LOWRIE MARSHALL

Close to the Heart
Dare to Be Happy
Aim for a Star
Hold to Your Dream

Bright Horizons

❧ ☙

HELEN LOWRIE MARSHALL

❧ ☙

Doubleday & Company, Inc.   Garden City, New York

Credit is given the Methodist Publishing Company and the Denver Post for permission to reprint certain poems in this book.

Library of Congress Catalog Card Number 54–37178
Copyright © 1954 by Helen Lowrie Marshall
All Rights Reserved
Printed in the United States of America

9 8 7 6 5 4 3

*To my husband
John Stanley Marshall*

and

*with grateful acknowledgment to
Jean and Vernon Coffey,
Dr. Harvey H. Potthoff
and all others who have helped
to make this book possible.*

Contents

Bright Horizons	9
Think On These Things	11
Silent Symphony	12
Thoughts In a Garden	13
Like a Patchwork Quilt	14
What Direction	15
The Humanist	16
No Regrets	17
Magnifying Glass	18
God's Symphony	19
Faith Grown Real	20
Along the Way	21
There Is a Force	22
And Wait on Thee	23
Give Us This Day	24
That Ye Might Have Life	25
"And I Work"	26
What Is Prayer?	27
Who Knows No Sacrifice	28
Self Searching	29
The Whispering of the Hours	30
And I Saw Not	31
Holy Ground	32
For Having Tried	33
The Fellow You Might Have Been	34
Yet Is There Hope	35
The Hard Way	36
God Must Have Known	37
By Any Other Name	38
My Altar	39
Rich Recompense	40

Like a Favorite Book	41
Heart-wise	42
The House You Call Home	43
But It Could Be	44
The Singer	45
We Pray	46
Beauty for Ashes	48
The Quest	49
Did They Know	50
A Fellow Needs	51
This I Do Pray	52
No Freedom	53
Little Things	54
Gratitude	56

Bright Horizons

*We should be glad for distant things,
For beauty 'round the bend;
For highways that lead on and on
With never any end.
Be glad for goals just out of reach,
The challenge of a star,
The glory of a distant light
That beckons from afar.
For hopes and dreams are built on
That enchanted distant mile,
And far off bright horizons
Make the road today worthwhile.*

Think On These Things

If you are ever plagued with doubt,
And question whether God's about,
Try thinking on some simple things;
You'll be surprised the peace it brings—
A sleeping child; a summer's day;
A puppy, awkward in its play;
The clean, washed air that follows rain;
A diamond-frosted window pane;
An apple tree all pink and white;
The stillness of a starlit night;
A fire crackling on the hearth;
The smell of freshly spaded earth;
A trail you knew once long ago;
A picket fence high-capped with snow;
A song your mother used to sing—
Why you can pick most anything
And you will find your answer there—
It's still God's world—He's everywhere!

Silent Symphony

Then must my thoughts to God be fenced with words?
Must love be couched in terms of a's and b's?
As well to score the music of the birds,
Or chart a stated course for every breeze.
No words can hold the ecstasies that start
Deep down within the temple of my heart,
As when I look upon my lilac tree
And prayer strikes up its silent symphony.

Thoughts In a Garden

Today, as I worked in my garden,
  I thought what a fine thing 'twould be
If each of us could pluck the weeds
  From our garden of memory.
If all of the harsh and ugly thoughts
  And every unkind deed
Could be tossed aside, and the barren spots
  Replaced with fresh new seed.

And I thought, if we could visualize
  The memories to grow
Out of the seeds we're planting—
  We'd live differently, I know;
We'd have more time for things worthwhile,
  The finer things, I'm sure,
And we'd plant the seed of a friendly smile
  Where a frown-weed grew before.

We'd give less thought to life's humdrum cares
  That seem to have no end,
And we'd learn the interest an hour bears
  When invested in a friend.
And oh, I know, if we could see—
  As true as stars above—
What tomorrow's memories would be,
  We'd have more time for love!

Like a Patchwork Quilt

Life isn't given us all of a piece;
   It's more like a patchwork quilt—
Each hour and minute a patch to fit in
   To the pattern that's being built.

With some patches gay—and some patches dark,
   And some that seem ever so dull—
But if we were given to set some apart,
   We'd hardly know which to cull.

For it takes the dark patches to set off the light,
   And the dull to show up the gay—
And, somehow, the pattern just wouldn't be right
   If we took any part away.

No, life isn't given us all of a piece,
   But in patches of hours to use,
That each might work out his own pattern of life
   To whatever design he choose.

What Direction

So you're running away from it all, you say?
Well, you're not the first one, son.
We, all of us, run away now and again—
The question is—WHERE do you run?

Do you follow the easier downhill course
Where you can just let yourself go,
With no better purpose than losing yourself
In the fog of the valley below?

Or do you try climbing away from it all?
The uphill road's tougher, that's true,
But, oh, it repays so much more than it costs
In its broader and finer view.

Yes, you can run downhill, or you can run up,
And either will take you as far—
But only a fool will bog down in the mud
When he can latch on to a star!

So don't let the fact that you're running away
Be of too much concern to you, son.
The running away doesn't matter so much—
It's in what direction you run!

The Humanist

"I'm not a praying man," he says,
   And quite believes it, too,
But you can always count on him
   When there is work to do;
He's right there with a helping hand
   Whenever there is need,
When there are children to be clothed
   Or hungry mouths to feed.

He's not a praying man, he says,
   And yet I've seen him share
With others, giving cheerfully,
   When he had none to spare;
I've heard him speak a kindly word
   When slander flew about,
And lend his quiet courage
   To the fellow down and out.

I've seen him watch a sunset,
   And listen to a song;
I've heard his friendly whistle
   When a stray dog came along—
Because of him, the world's
   A little better place today—
And yet he quite believes it
   When he says he doesn't pray!

No Regrets

Never regret a ride on a star,
A dream, or a hope that was aimed too far;
That wonderful castle you built in the air,
Though it tumbled and left but a memory there.
For dreams that go drifting,
And hopes that are high—
A ride on a star through a silvery sky—
These are the wonderful, magical things,
These are the glorious, gossamer wings
That carry us up where the angels play,
And Heaven is ours—though it's only a day;
But one day in Heaven has infinite worth
In brightening the practical pathways of earth.

Magnifying Glass

How many of us go through life
   With a magnifying glass,
Doubling and tripling our troubles,
   Reluctant to let them pass;

Magnifying our daily lot
   Of worry and toil and care
'Til they become almost too great
   A load for us to bear.

But how many times do we think to hold
   That glass that magnifies
Over the little joys we know
   And tripling their size?

For joys, too, are what we make of them,
   Whether they're large or small.
It's surprising, sometimes, the blessings we find
   If we look for them at all!

And we can control the size of our joys,
   As well as the size of our woes—
It all depends how we hold the glass
   Whether trouble or happiness grows.

God's Symphony

God plays His symphony
Upon the heartstrings—yours and mine;
With gentle, knowing touch
He weaves His harmony divine;
And if, sometimes, harsh discord
Makes that harmony unfair,
If war and strife and bitterness
Confuse the peaceful air,
'Tis not God's lack of artistry
Nor symphony grown dim,
But, rather, that our hearts have fallen
Out of tune with Him.

Faith Grown Real

I said that I believed—not hard to say
When all about me bloomed a summer day.
When life was all aglow with warmth and light,
Small wonder that my faith waxed gay and bright;
For who could doubt a God who made the flowers
And filled each sunny day with happy hours?

But one day I awoke to find the snow
Had covered all my world. I didn't know
That life could be so cold or skies so grey.
The sun and God were hidden quite away
And faith was dead—nor any shallow prayer
I might have said could ever make it fair.

As surely as the flowers that had bloomed
But yesterday, so was my fine faith doomed.
Barren and brown it lay, a lifeless thing—
Or so I thought—but I'd forgotten spring.
There came a day when winter's snows were past
And there I found my faith grown real at last.

Along the Way

We cannot all be ministers
And preach with learned phrase;
Nor can we all be soloists
With golden song of praise;
But we can live a sermon here
And we can live a song,
And neither song nor sermon
Need be either loud or long;
But quietly, in little things
We do from day to day—
Some simple, kindly deed,
Some word of comfort we may say—
And, even though we're unaware
That such has been our goal,
Somewhere along the way an angel
Writes, "He saved a soul!"

There Is a Force

There is a Force that spurs me on,
   And will not let me rest—
Some Destiny demands I climb
   Forever toward the crest.

There is a seething, surging Urge
   That will not let me sleep
'Til I have scaled the heights of high
   And probed the depths of deep.

There is a Light that leads me on,
   Though darkness hide my sun;
There is a Hand that lifts me up
   When I would fain have done.

There is a Dream that beckons me
   Ever to hills beyond;
There is a Song that will not still;
   A Hope reborn each dawn.

There is a Faith that will not die,
   Though put to storm and test;
There is a Force—could it be God?—
   That draws from me—my best.

And Wait on Thee

We pray, "Lord, these things we desire."
And then expect them to transpire
At once. We cannot see the way
That God must work. We merely pray,
And, puzzled, fail to understand
Why every petty small demand
Is not fulfilled forthwith. We say,
"If it be true that God is there,
Why, then, does He not answer prayer?"
Oh, of so little faith are we!
So small we are, we cannot see
The farflung ways God shapes our ends.
Our small mind only comprehends
The very near for which we yearn.
Oh, that we all might better learn
More patience—faith—that we might be
Willing to wait, dear Lord, on Thee!

Give Us This Day

God of forgotten ones everywhere,
Friend of the fatherless, hear our prayer—
We ask so little—not fame, nor wealth,
Nor even happiness, nor health.
We only ask that we be fed—
"Give us this day our daily bread."

Father of all the orphaned ones,
We, who were born to the sound of guns,
Upon whose shoulders, frail, must bear
The world's grim weight of want and care;
We pray now, as the Master said—
"Give us this day our daily bread."

God of the world, if Thou would touch
The hearts of those who have so much;
Help them to see the empty hands
Reaching to them from war-torn lands.
By Thy great mercy may they be led—
"Give us this day our daily bread."

That Ye Might Have Life

Abundant life—the precious gift
   Thou gavest, Lord, to me—
Shall I but lift the wrappings, then,
   And merely look to see
What manner gift was given thus,
   Then wrap and store away,
Hoarding against the greater need
   Of some far distant day?

Oh no, Lord—let me see and hear
   And feel and taste and know
The full, rich goodness of this gift
   Thy bounty dost bestow;
The joyous zest of living—
   This gift Thou gavest me—
Then let me laugh and love and live,
   Dear Lord—abundantly!

"And I Work"

Pity the man who has no work to do,
Sorry, indeed, is he, when day is through,
Who cannot find it in himself to say,
"So much have I accomplished through this day."

With all my heart I pity him who lives
Never to know the joy true labor gives—
Never to know that satisfying rest
That comes to those who've given of their best.

"My Father worketh," so the Master said,
"My Father worketh—and I work,"—and led
His little band of workers day by day,
Doing whatever tasks might fall their way.

Oh, blest is he who follows where He trod,
Who's learned the love of labor—and of God—
For he who knows the simple dignity
Of service—wealthy in content is he!

What Is Prayer?

What is prayer?—Appreciation
And sincere evaluation
Of the finer things of life
   Along the way.
It's a quality of living
With a quantity of giving,
And a blessed sense of peace
   At close of day.

It's believing—and not grieving,
It's achieving; and receiving
With a thankful heart the blessings
   God bestows;
It's the silent thanks inside you
When the grievances that tried you
Have been downed with patience, rather
   Than with blows.

What is prayer?—a deep conviction
That belies all contradiction,
That no matter where you are
   God, too, is there.
It's that quiet heart's awareness
Of the beauty and the fairness
Of this world of God's and ours—
   That is prayer.

Who Knows No Sacrifice

God pity him who knows no sacrifice,
Whose heart has never paid a precious price.
He does not live
Who's never felt the warming fire
Of love, transcending all desire
Save but to give.

Self Searching

A part of me I own, but only part;
There still are deep recesses in my heart,
And vast uncharted wastelands in my mind
I must explore, and search until I find
The rest of me; when I possess my soul,
Then—then will I be whole.

The Whispering of the Hours

It's a fancy of mine—and a foolish one, too,
But I like to imagine that when the day's through
And darkness has settled and all is at rest,
That the hours come gathering for a talk-fest,
And they whisper among themselves all that has passed
From the very first hour of dawn to the last.

And sometimes their whisp'rings have made me right glad
To think I'd accomplished the things that I had—
And sometimes the hours embarrass me quite
With the things that I didn't get done, that I might.
And often some hours have nothing to say—
Poor, frail, little hours—quite wasted away!
While others are packed fairly ready to burst—
But each tells his tale, from the best to the worst,
And I lie there and listen while they whisper on
Till—all without warning—it's dawn, and they're gone!

And I Saw Not

I watched the sunset with my eyes,
  Spoke lightly of its beauty;
And to the poor gave with my hands,
  Believing it my duty.
I heard rare music with my ears,
  Politely murmured praises;
And from my lips took care there passed
  The proper social phrases.

I thought that I was living—
  That life was full and sweet—
But when night's darkness found my soul
  It knew no safe retreat.
My clutching fingers found no faith,
  My feet no solid ground;
In empty words and hollow mirth
  No comfort could be found.

Then, somehow, through the dark of night
  I saw the stars above,
And somehow, God came into sight,
  And somehow, I found love.
Then music, friendship, giving—
  All these things I understood;
I watched the sunrise with my heart
  And knew that life was good!

Holy Ground

On what divergent paths man seeks the heights.
How many different roadways has he trod
Upward and ever up, since time began,
His face turned to the Sun and Stars—and God.

And wise is he who sees the worth of all,
For beauty lies in all ways men have found.
And none is perfect, none without a flaw—
Yet every pathway there—is Holy Ground.

For Having Tried

I'm such a little person, Lord, though long
I've held my head and shoulders high—stood tall,
Borne burdens never meant for one not strong—
Deep down inside I've had no strength at all.

My soul has flinched at each new load I've borne
And, oh, the many secret times I've cried;
Yet always, somehow, I must carry on,
In tribute to my self, my love, my pride.

I've dared not let the world, and those I love,
Surmise how weak and helpless, these my hands,
And so I've drawn false strength on like a glove,
And with a calm, unfelt, met life's demands.

But knowing, Lord, how small I am inside,
And though You see the pretense and the sham,
Please—give me just one mark for having tried
To be a bigger person than I am.

The Fellow You Might Have Been

Did you ever think what you might have been
  If you'd never a bruise or scar?
It's the rougher ways and the tougher days
  That have made you the man you are.

The closer a vine's cut back sometimes,
  The finer and stronger it grows;
Who knows—if you'd never been pricked by
    the thorns,
  You might never have known the rose.

You may think Fate's handed you more than
    your share,
  And maybe it's hard to grin,
But the chances are you're a better man
  Than the fellow you might have been.

Yet Is There Hope

Men talk of war—we hear them say
That wars can never cease.
Men talk of war—but when they pray,
They pray for Peace.

Men talk of war—we see them build
Their strength against the day
When war shall come—but yet 'tis Peace
For which they pray.

Men talk of war, the nations warn
For war we must prepare—
Yet is there hope so long as Peace
Shall be man's prayer.

The Hard Way

A man can be good,
Live the way that he should,
Be generous, ready to give;
He can do what is right,
Keep his name free from blight,
An exemplary life he can live;
He may die quite content
Never knowing what's meant
By the fine fellowship of God's people;
He can live his life through—
And many folks do—
Quite ignoring the sign of the steeple:
His ideals can be true,
He can follow them, too,
He can fight for the right with all ardor;
He can be a fine man,
We admit that he can,
Outside of the church—
But it's harder!

God Must Have Known

God must have known how we would need
Some dear one close at hand;
Someone that we could count on,
Who would always understand;

Someone whose love would rise above
Our faults—our negligence;
One who would know no sacrifice—
Expect no recompense.

God must have known that other loves,
Though precious they might be,
Could never quite fulfill this
Special need of you and me.

He must have known that sometimes, too,
We'd need a gentle prod,
A quiet close reminder of
The constant love of God.

God must have known we'd need one love,
Steadfast above all others,
A love more likened to His own—
And that's why He made Mothers.

By Any Other Name

To seek the heights and depths of thought
 And pause in silence there;
Some call it meditation—
 I like to call it prayer.

To look out on the troubled world
 And find the true and fair;
Some call it contemplation—
 I like to call it prayer.

To give oneself for others,
 To lift and love and share,
Some call it consecration—
 I like to call it prayer.

To sense a silent, reverent awe
 At beauty everywhere;
Some call it adoration—
 I like to call it prayer.

My Altar

I have a little altar in my heart—
A corner set aside, a shrine apart;
And oh, a dozen times or more a day
I find me stealing quietly away
To kneel before my little altar there
And offer up a thought or two in prayer—
A little "Thank you, God" when things
  go right;
A prayer for light to guide me thru the night;
A plea for strength to help me right the wrong;
Or sometimes, maybe, just a bit of song.
I have a little altar in my heart—
A corner set aside, a shrine apart,
A quiet place where I find sweet release
From daily care—and strength and joy
  and peace.

Rich Recompense

So many crumpled dreams a-down the years,
So many hopes and ideals crushed and bruised—
Yet, somehow, through the heartache and the tears
Were salvaged odds and ends that might be used.

A bit of wisdom picked up here and there,
Some depth of understanding I'd not known,
Had I not paid the price of tear and care,
Had I not, too, once suffered all alone.

A little light—scarce more than candle gleam—
To pierce the darkness that beset me so,
And yet a light, to shed its tiny beam
And help me find the better way to go.

Just odds and ends redeemed from yesterday—
But, somehow, out of that conglomerate whole
That, through God's grace, I had not tossed away,
A miracle emerged—I found my soul.

Like a Favorite Book

Sometimes a friend is like a favorite book;
You know his every thought and word and look—
And yet you like him handy on your shelf,
Because, somehow, he warms your deeper self.

He may not hold the thrill that others do,
But just because he's genuine and true,
Like some fine masterpiece beyond compare,
When all the rest are gone, he'll still be there.

Yes, some friends are a lot like favorite books;
They don't depend upon their fame or looks.
It's what's inside—their deeper basic worth—
That makes us hold some friends the best on earth.

Heart-wise

True wisdom of the heart comes precious high,
The smallest bit is worth at least a sigh;
And only those who've known a love and lost,
Can know how many tears such wisdom cost.

At such a price of grief and pain and tears
These hearts of ours grow wiser through the years;
A bitter price—so oft not understood—
Yet I think we'd not change it if we could.

For with each bit of wisdom it has known,
We find the heart has deeper, warmer grown.
Our life is strangely richer for each loss—
And resurrection follows still the cross.

The House You Call Home

May the house you call home
Have sturdy walls,
And windows that face the sun;
With doors that swing wide
With a welcome inside
To warm you when day is done.

May the echo of laughter
Resound from each rafter,
And peace and contentment dwell there.
May the house you call home
Be a haven of rest,
Secure 'neath a roof of prayer.

But It Could Be

I know not if this prayer of mine
   To bless one far away,
Will bring to him the good things
   I would ask for him today.
I know the Master knows, far more
   Than I, his every need,
And, in His wisdom, will or will not
   Grant the things I plead.

But it could be that in some way—
   Some Heaven-born way, divine,
My very wish for blessings asked
   Will reach this friend of mine.
Perhaps some hidden, unknown wave
   Will carry on its crest
Across the sea of time and space
   My wish that he be blessed.

And even though God may not choose
   To grant this special plea,
Because of it, perhaps, my friend
   Will catch a smile from me.
Perhaps some bit of happiness
   Will somehow find its way
To warm the heart of him because
   I prayed for him today.

The Singer

She cheerily vowed she'd no time to pray,
So many homely tasks took up her day—
But I can still remember well the song
She sang about her work the whole day long—
A simple, little tune with nonsense rhyme,
Her broom, or mop, or scrub-brush keeping time—
But we, whose privilege it was to be
Where we could hear that cheery melody,
Found our world brighter as we went along,
Humming remembered snatches of her song—
And God, I know, smiled down upon her there,
Whose foolish, little song was really prayer.

We Pray

Lord of the nations all, we pray;
A sick, bewildered world today,
Groping our way in darkness, we
Have need of light that we may see;
Have need of truth, that we may know
The right, the sure, safe way to go.

Lord of the nations all, we plead
Forgiveness in our hour of need.
So many weary miles we've trod
On paths that lead away from God—
So many manmade plans we've tried,
So many of our sons have died—
So many schemes to no account,
When just the Sermon on the Mount,
Had we but listened, would have spared
This suffering the world has shared.

Lord of the nations all, hold high
The light of truth against the sky.
Perhaps we are not yet too blind
The path of righteousness to find,
The power of love to understand—
And then, if Thou wilt take our hand
And guide us, lest we stray again,
We shall find rest and peace—
                              Amen.

Beauty for Ashes

Have you ever felt the walls of life
Come tumbling round your ears?
Have you ever sickened with the weight
Of countless untold fears?
Have you watched your candlelight of faith
Grow dim when hope was gone,
And have you felt that all was night
With never any dawn,
And there was nothing left to pin
Your dreams and wishes on?
    I have.

But then I've seen a crocus
Pushing through the winter's snow;
And I have watched a tiny,
Tender seedling start to grow;
And I have seen the dry earth
Spring to life and bloom again
Beneath the magic of a cool,
Refreshing summer rain—
And I've found, though I've no balm
To heal the hopelessness and pain—
    God has.

The Quest

The Mind strides forth in search of truth and right,
Brandishing high the penetrating light
Of Reason, in all earnestness to find
The goal eternal of all humankind;
Seeking some hidden pathway yet untrod,
That shall reveal a proven, living God.

But deep within its templed walls, the Heart
Knows that the quest must end back at its start.
Serene, it lights Love's candles on the sill,
Content to bide its quiet time until
The brilliant light of Reason finds its way
Back, to suffuse with Love's own warmer ray;
Until the weary Mind shall turn once more
Back to the Heart's own gentle, open door,
To learn its very quest would not have been
Had not the God it sought dwelt close within.

Did They Know

He took God with him
  To work today,
And no one else knew it, of course—
  Or did they?

Could they sense it, I wonder,
  In various ways
That made this day different
  From other work days?

Could they tell it, perhaps,
  In the warmth of his smile
That, somehow, made even
  The dull tasks worthwhile?

Could they feel how the calm
  From that great, hidden Source
Radiated its strength
  Through the whole office force?

Did they know their small grievances
  Melted away
All because he took God to work
  With him today?

A Fellow Needs

A fellow needs so very much
   To feel that he belongs;
To feel he has some spot to call
   His own amid life's throngs.

A fellow needs so very much
   To have someone who cares—
Someone to share his joys as well
   As burdens that he bears.

A fellow needs so very much
   To know he fills a part
That no one else could quite fulfill
   Within some dear one's heart.

This I Do Pray

I cannot pray for this or that to happen;
God's will divine is not so simply swayed.
I can but hope—for hope is ours always,
And pray, whatever comes, that we be made
Strong in the strength that He alone can give us
To meet the hoped-for or the dreaded day.
I cannot pray for this or that to happen,
But, oh, for courage, Lord, this I do pray.

No Freedom

There is no freedom—man is only free
To choose his master. If a slave is he
To Power, Wealth—or Envy, Hate and Greed,
Then galling will he find his bonds, indeed;

But he, who 'slaves his willing heart to Love,
Though strong the links his chains be
  fashioned of,
Shall find his soul content, nor seeks release
For Love, alone, gives liberty—and peace.

Little Things

Dear God, please give to me
A thankful heart for little things—
For sunshine on my kitchen floor,
For news the postman brings;
For memories in the making,
Things the children do and say,
That I will smile about, perhaps,
Some future, lonelier day.

Grant me appreciation
Of the small joys that are mine—
The children's birthday parties,
My honeysuckle vine;
The clean, fresh smell
Of clothes just washed;
The ivy on my wall,
The children's thrilled delight
To wake and find the first snowfall.
For robins in the springtime,
And autumn's crispy weather—
For leaves that crunch;
Friends in for lunch
And laughter shared together.

Give me enthusiasm
To greet each brand new day
With an honest joy in living
As I go my simple way;
I do not ask contentment
That would ambition stay—
But let me love the little things
I find along the way.

Gratitude

"How can I ever repay you?"
I've said it, and so have you.
How can I ever in all this world
Repay the things you do?

Perhaps I never can repay
To you—or you to me,
But we can pass that kindness on
To others we may see.

And though you never need my help—
I pray you never do—
By helping others, I'll repay
My heartfelt debt to you.